WHOOSH! WENT THE WISH

TOBY SPEED

ILLUSTRATED BY **BARRY ROOT**

G. P. PUTNAM'S SONS ▾ NEW YORK

Printed in Hong Kong by South China Printing Co. (1988) Ltd.

Designed by Gunta Alexander. Text set in Berkeley Old Style.

The art was done in gouache, watercolor,

and Conté on Arches 100 lb. hot press.

Library of Congress Cataloging-in-Publication Data

Speed, Toby. Whoosh! went the wish/Toby Speed; illustrated by Barry Root.

p.   cm.   Summary: All Henry wants is a cat, and when the

mountain fairy finally grants his wish she grants a wish of her

own at the same time. [1. Fairies—Fiction. 2. Wishes—Fiction.

3. Cats—Fiction.] I. Root, Barry, ill. II. Title.   PZ7.S746115Wh   1997

[E]—dc20   95-10592   CIP   AC   ISBN 0-399-23000-9

1 3 5 7 9 10 8 6 4 2

First Impression

To Audrey, heart of my heart—T.S.

For Gwynn—B.R.

Henry's house had four windows, from which he could see the whole world. He saw the forest to the east. He saw the ocean to the west. He saw the meadow to the south. He saw the mountain to the north. But Henry had lived alone for more years than a pomegranate has seeds, and he was lonely.

Every morning Henry looked out his east window and
said, "I wish I had a cat. A cat would be such pleasant
company." But no cat came.

At noon he looked out his west window and said, "I wish I had a cat. A cat on a summer day would be just the thing to keep the bugs away." But no cat came.

In the evening he looked out his south window and said, "Oh, how I wish I had a cat! A cat on a winter night would be just the thing to warm my lonesome lap." But no cat came.

By nightfall Henry was too tired to wish. He looked out his north window toward the big mountain—and fell asleep.

In the city lived a fairy who was fed up with the wishing business. And with good reason!

All day she waved her wand, granting wishes to passersby. But people wished for the silliest things. Some of them wished the light would change. Others wished for taxis. *I'm in a rut*, thought the fairy. So when the mountain became available, she moved.

But her old city customers were faithful and followed her to the mountain. All she got were long-distance wishes from people who were too busy to shop. They sent their chauffeurs over in limousines to deliver their wishes. Or they dropped tiny envelopes from helicopters.

It was a thankless job—except for Henry. Henry was sincere. Even though the fairy was too far away to hear his wish, she could see how shiny it was.

Day after day she watched wishes fly from Henry's lips like silent silver birds, fly in every direction but hers. All those wishes going to waste!

At last she went down to see him.

"Face the mountain when you wish," she announced. "You'll get it in a trice."

Henry laughed softly. "I never heard a fairy ask for wishes," he said, but when she had gone he faced the mountain and said, "Far and away, above all else, I wish for a cat."

that was real

Whooooosh! went the wish. But on the way the last two words got stuck in the branches of a bongololly tree. *Zing!* went the fairy's wand. She watched in amazement as the wish sailed over her head, then over the mountaintop and up into the clouds—far and away and above all else. Down the mountain she skipped.

"Try again," she told Henry. "That one got away." And back up she went.

FAR AND AWAY

So Henry wished again. "A cat is all I want, to fill my house."

Whooooosh! went the wish. But on the way a gust of wind caught the first four words and blew them into a bramble bush, where they stuck. *Zing!* went the fairy's wand, granting the rest of the wish. Down the mountain she skipped.

I WANT TO FILL MY HOUSE

A CAT IS ALL

"Mountain fairy!" shouted Henry. "Just look at my house. All I wished for was a cat, and I have no room for that."

"I didn't hear anything about a cat," said the fairy. "But your house is certainly filled."

And indeed it was. Every nook and niche and cranny and corner was crowded and crammed with stuff.

There were highboys, lowboys,
davenports, and antimacassars.
Pots and pans and calabashes.
Dish racks and bric-a-brac.
Sideboards, cutting boards,
scrubbing boards, and diving boards.
Rocking chairs, wing chairs,
scrunching-down-for-snoozing chairs.
Pie pans, frying pans,
soaking pans, and boiling pans.
Resting pillows, nesting pillows,
tossing-up-and-throwing pillows.
Every alcove had a stove.
Every hat rack had a hat.
But no cat.

"Don't worry," said the fairy.
"I can fix this. Wish again." And back
up the mountain she went.

So Henry wished again. "I want nothing but a cat."
Whooooosh! went the wish. But on the way a jutting rock caught the last three words and knocked them into a brier patch, where they stuck. *Zing!* went the fairy's wand, granting the rest of the wish. Down the mountain she skipped.

BUT I

WANT NOTHING

A

CAT

"Mountain fairy!" cried Henry. "Now look what you've done. I have nothing."

And indeed Henry had absolutely nothing—not even his house.

"Well, you wished for nothing," scoffed the fairy.
"Nothing but a cat! Now what shall I do?"
"Wait," said the fairy. "I can fix this."

Up the mountain she went, fuming. "Old hill," she muttered, "find yourself another fairy. I wish Henry had his house back. And I wish I were his cat."

Zing! went her wand, and this time both wishes came true, every scrap and syllable. Down the mountain she went.

"What a beautiful cat!" said Henry, picking her up.
The fairy cat just purred in his arms.

The next day Henry was a happy man in the middle
of the world. He looked out his four windows and said,
"Thank you, dear mountain fairy, wherever you are."
    On his lap the fairy cat purred and purred. She had
gotten her wish, too.